Arnold Isler

Wild Thoughts in Rhyme

Arnold Isler

Wild Thoughts in Rhyme

ISBN/EAN: 9783337270308

Printed in Europe, USA, Canada, Australia, Japan

Cover: Foto ©Andreas Hilbeck / pixelio.de

More available books at **www.hansebooks.com**

WILD THOUGHTS IN RHYME.

BY

PRESS OF SMYTHE & CO.,
COLUMBUS, OHIO.

PREFACE.

THE rhymes in this volume may be thought to possess little or no merit, but verse making has not been, neither is it, the chief pursuit of my life. An infant exile from my native hills of Switzerland at the early age of five years; a runaway and "street arab" at nine; a soldier boy in the 23rd Ohio Infantry at twelve; without a home, friends or means, I grew up untaught, unlettered, and without culture. Knowing no art but the promptings of a wild, wayward nature, I rhymed, perhaps, without reason, and because I had nothing else to do that I liked better. I claim no further merit than that I have written with all simplicity, and according to ability and opportunity.

I am very much indebted to my kind friends LUKE G. BYRNE, CAPT. GEO. CUNNINGHAM, and DAVID WELLING, for generous aid extended toward the formation and publication of this work.

A. I.

TO KATE.

ESTERDAY, wandering with shoeless feet,
 A runaway, facing the wind's cold blast;
 And with the ragabonds who haunt the street—
With all that was villianous I was class'd;
The world look'd on me as a lost outcast;
 Scorn'd me, mock'd me, but never tried to cheer
My sadden'd heart; people hastily pass'd
 Where I stood, as if they were in fear
 That I might cry for help if they lingered near.

And while the world saw me in deep despair,
 Miserable and wretched, yet would not move
One single step to aid me—thou didst dare
 To meet the world's scorn for me; thou sweet dove
Did'st dare to give to me thy virgin love,
 When others would not e'en approach me near;
Thou dared to smile for me when all above
 Was darkness; with thy voice charmingly clear,
 Thou raised my sinking heart with sweet words of cheer.

Thou did'st not shun the dark-eyed stranger,
 Altho' thy nearest friends bade thee " beware ;"
Thou wast too innocent to fear the danger
 That others feared ; thy heart was free from care,
And thou could'st not see me lost in despair ;
 So thou didst sing for me enchanting lays,
That thrilled me with their sweetness rich and rare ;
 While smiles 'yond the pow'r of my rhymes to praise,
 With justice, beam'd for me on thy beautiful face.

To-day this life of mine seems wondrous bright,
 The world that look'd so dark but yesterday—

Has met with sudden change; and now the light
  Of Heaven shines lustrously o'er my way.
I need not now with shoeless feet to stray,
  Or brave the storm in some lone, dismal street—
I have comforts now to make life dear; yea,
  And friends seek me now in my own retreat,
  And Love and Friendship me with pleasures greet.

But Kate, this change of fortune cannot move me;
  My soul's thoughts, my heart's love—all that is mine,
I have most willingly resigned to thee;
  Tho' other faces be as fair as thine,
Tho' other eyes may just as brightly shine,
  Tho' other lips may be as sweet to press,
And other hearts give love as pure, divine,
  Yet, darling Kate, I am thine, thine to bless,
  Thy true companion thro' the world's wide wilderness.

O, I love thee! I love those hazel eyes
  That thrill me with their love-glances for me;
Those bewitching smiles of thine I prize
  Far above the rarest gems of the sea;
But that forgiving spirit born in thee,
  I prize above all thy other charms; thou art
My heart's choice, and evermore will be
  Nearest to me; my love will never part
  From thee, but will fore'er find peace within thy heart.

I am thine, wife, love, thine forevermore;
  And thou art mine, and we are two in one;
Let winds blow wild, let thunders loudly roar,
  Let rains pour down and in deep torrents run;
Let thick darkness come, let the proud red sun
  Hide behind the black clouds; ha! what care we?
We'll cling together till life's task is done—
  Thro' sorrow and pleasure, no odds what, be
  Two in one, thro' all life, thro' all eternity.

CONTENTS.

Wild Thoughts in Rhyme.

THE LAMENT.

HOURS pass drearily,
Slowly, uncheerily,
Passes the day;
Life now seems drear to me,
She who was dear to me,
Faithful, sincere to me,
Has pass'd away.

To come back nevermore—
To rest forevermore—
In realms above.
Why did death come so soon?
Strike my love dumb so soon?
Ah, me! leave numb so soon,
My darling love?

THE LAMENT.

O! she was beautiful,
Gentle and dutiful,
    Heart full of cheer;
Sang songs deliciously,
Acted judiciously,
Life passed auspiciously,
    Till death came near.

Took my sweetheart away,
My life's best part away,
    All that I adore.
All that gave cheer to me,
All that was dear to me,
All that was near to me,
    But near no more.

O! I would death was nigh,
That my last breath was nigh,
    That life was o'er:
For day is now night to me,
Eyes that gave light to me,

THE LAMENT.

And shone so bright for me,
　Will shine no more.

But why here weeping now?
Angels are keeping now,
　My love so fair;
In that sweet land of love,
Where that bright band of love,
Ruled by command of love,
　Dwells free from care.

Onward I'll roam each day,
Nearer that home each day,
　That Elysian shore;
Where I will meet my love,
Joyously greet my love,
Be with thee, sweet, my love,
　Forevermore.

I, WHO am I? Why, myself—*Me!*
   Well, who is me? Why myself—I!
I, that is me.   Now I see
   Thro' it. I'm getting nigh
The point.   I am! I know this to be
   A fact.   I am what?
Ah! there it is.   I am what? I see
   And still I do not.
Yet I do know I am; 'tis a great treat
  To know so much. To know I am a thing,
A living thing, that lives thro' bitter and sweet,
  For what? That's it, for what? I talk, I sing,
I feel, I hear, I see, I laugh, I weep;
I love, I hate, I work, I play, I sleep;
And in my sleep I dream. In dreams I see

Strange things, strange scenes, strange faces appear
       to me;
I wake, and lo! I find myself where I
Was before I courted sleep. I sigh,
I rise, I eat, I drink, I live, I die!
Then what?
        Ah! there it is:
What not—
       'Cross Death's abyss!
Another life like this?
        God forbid!
I would rather forevermore lie hid
In Earth's cold clay, forever senseless, dead!
Than live another life like this, and tread
Again the rough, changing pathway of life,
Brave over again this mixed up mystic strife.

WASTE as you will your hours of leisure.
  You young folks, low and high,
No doubt you all have some sweet pleasure.
  On which you do rely;
But there is nothing half so pleasant,—
  That is to Jane and I,—
When we know there's no one present,
  As "kissing on the sly."

Now, Jane's mother does not believe in
  This "kissing on the sly;"
She thinks young men are so deceiving,
  Girls ought to be more shy!
But Jane, like me, can't see the harm in
  (When no one else is nigh),

KISSING ON THE SLY.

Kissing. Oh! it is so charming,
　　This "kissing on the sly."

'Sides, Jane and I have many reasons
　　For "kissing on the sly;"
'Tis just as good in all the seasons,
　　Be seasons wet or dry;
It don't play out like other pleasures,
　　Nor need we to apply
To any keen and severe measures,
　　For "kissing on the sly."

When Jane's mother is down the cellar,
　　And no one else is nigh,
Jane looks roguishly at her fellow,
　　Meaning, "How's this for high?"
While I, you see, draw somewhat nearer
　　To this maiden so shy,
For well I know that naught can cheer her,
　　As "kissing on the sly."

Time passes fast; Jane and I soon will be
  Tied together by that tie
Called the wedlock tie, but we'll still be
  Innocently, Jane and I ;
And though some of life's joys may perish
  As the years go gliding by,
Yet there is one we'll ever cherish—
  'Tis "kissing on the sly."

THE POOR.

D<small>AY</small> after day
    Toiling away,
To fill the rich man's treasure,
To give him wealth and pleasure.
Ah! but small is the measure,
    Little the pay,
That the poor man gets for toiling
    Day after day.

    Stitch after stitch,
    Sewing for the rich,
All the long day so dreary,
In her cot, lone, uncheery,
With fingers, sore, weary,
    Sewing away,

THE POOR.

Poor woman sewing for the wealthy,
    Day after day.

    Work, work away!
    Day after day.
What care "we rich" for the poor?
What's it to us what they endure
From misfortunes and troubles? Sure,
    We give them pay;
Besides kicks, threats, and curses,
    Day after day.

    O God! defend
    The poor, befriend
Them in the hour of trouble.
Let not their sorrows double,
Let not their bright hopes bubble
    Into despair;
Keep them, O Father! forever,
    Under Thy care.

MY GIRL.

PRETTIEST.
  Wittiest,
Among all the girls:
  The sweetest,
  The neatest,
More precious than pearls.

  Industr'ous,
  Not blustrous,
But modest and kind;
  She's spareful,
  She's careful,
And all right in mind.

  She faints not,
  She paints not,

Like some foolish girls;

She pouts not,

She spouts not,

Because her hair curls.

Not childish,

Not wildish,

Not running here, there;

Not frettish,

Coquettish,

Like some young girls are.

Not wealthy,

But healthy,

And alarmingly smart.

A dandy

With candy

Can not win her heart.

CUBA.

Hark! do you hear the war-like tramping?
　　Hark! do you hear the church bells ringing!
Sons of Cuba on mountains camping,
　　Daughters of Cuba in valleys singing,
　　　　"For Liberty make way!"

Each day brings news of a battle!
　　Thro'out the Isle the war flags are flying!
Thro'out the Isle the loud cannons rattle!
　　Thro'out the Isle the poor slaves are crying
　　　　"For Liberty make way!"

O, ye heavens, so bright and serene!
　　　　What does this mean,
　　　　This terrific war scene?
This shower of blood on the fields so green?

This cry for revenge from the tongues of slaves?
This sudden gathering of Cuba's braves?
This meeting of armies on hill and plain?
This grand uprising against the powers of Spain?

What does it mean? It means death to all
Who dare to fight against freedom, and enthrall
Human beings whom the Almighty made
Out of the same dust, tho' of a different shade:
For Liberty is now leading the school,
That long has suffered 'neath priestly rule:
It means that the tyrants over the main,
Have no right in America to reign!
It means that rather than to live a slave,
And die to be laid in an unmarked grave,
A true spirited man will willingly brave—
And fight with zeal unconquerable—
The combined elements of earth and hell.

Americans! stand ye not idle to-day!
Push with your arms to the shore of Cuba.

Go, and fight for them who for freedom fight.

Help them defend what is noble and right.

And to thee—O, Goddess of Liberty !

March on, forever victoriously.

And damned be he,

Whoever he may be,

That ventures to raise a sword against thee.

MAY, 1869.

EPIGRAM.

ON A CRITIC.

HE deems himself wise, a master in the world's
    grand school ;

He calls my rhymes the thoughts of a silly
    young elf ;

A wise man can not criticise the works of a fool,

Without making a fool of himself.

THE BEAUTIFUL GIRLS.

OH, the girls, the beautiful girls!
  With their laughing eyes and dancing curls:
How they bewitch us by day and by night,
How they cause our hearts to beat with delight,
Pleasing,
        Teasing,
            Charming creatures!
Bewitching smiles brightening their features;
How can they deceive us, as ofttimes they do,
With sweet glowing words and eyes of bright blue?

How dearly we prize the beautiful girls,
Far above rubies, diamonds or pearls!
How delighted we feel whenever we meet

The pretty, loved ones on the busy street,

Walking,

       Talking,

            Smiling so sweet,

Dressed in dresses made exquisitely neat:

But it beats the Old Harry what a big price

"We men" have to pay for those dresses so nice.

Oh, the girls, the beautiful girls!

How we love to finger their dancing curls;

How we love to see roses, fresh and sweet,

Bloom on their cheeks, while Love's moments fleet:

Cooing,

       Wooing,

            Evening hours away,

Little dreaming of the coming day;

Kissing is sweet, and squeezing is sport—

Who wouldn't be a member of Cupid's court?

Oh! it's strange how our beautiful girls

Have got into the habit of shaking their curls,

And smiling, whenever they chance to meet

A fancy-dressed fop on the busy street;
Winking,
       Blinking,
             Flirting away;
Ostentously walking the streets all day;
Dear, innocent girls! "just out on a lark—
Who cares for mother—we'll be home before dark."

Once I fell in love with a beautiful girl,
With pretty black eyes, that would snap and whirl;
And soft, warm cheeks, never stained with paint,
And lips—by the god's! they'd tempt a saint;
Daily,
       Gayly,
             My bonnie Jane!
Met me at the end of the old farm lane;
Fondly embraced 'neath a chestnut tree—
Earth was Elysium when she was with me!

The sweetest scenes in life will ofttimes change
To the bitterest; so you'll not deem it strange
If I should tell you, in a deacon-like way,

That on one delectable summer day

My love,

  My dove,

    My innocent Jane!

Left her home to follow a circus-train;

Oh, Cupid! how couldst thou so cruelly seize

My love, to mount her on the dizzy trapeze?

Still, I love the beautiful girls!

With their laughing eyes and dancing curls,

And go I through pleasure, and go I through woe,

I will think of them wherever I go;

Dearly,

  Sincerely,

    My heart does beat

For the lasses, so lovely, and good, and sweet;

Bewitching creatures, more precious then pearls—

A fig for earth without the beautiful girls!

LEAVING silent chamber
  For the sylvan lawn;
Viewing Nature's beauties
  At the break of dawn;
For Nature seemeth fairest,
  (So the poets say):
Loveliest and liveliest,
  At the break of day.

Listening to the murmurs
  Of waters flowing by;
Beautiful deep river!
  Clear as a maiden's eye;
Merrily and cheerfully,
  Rippling away;

Everything seemeth lively
At the break of day.

Listening to the song-birds,
So full of love and cheer;
Flitting through the branches,
Ofttimes flitting near.
Deliciously caroling
Morning hours away;
Everything seemeth lively
At the break of day.

Listen, birds, oh, listen!
Some sweet voice I hear;
Yes, it is my darling,
Coming, coming near!
Pretty, dark-eyed Katie,
Ever blithe and gay,
Singing in the morning,
At the break of day.

Halloo! here is Rover,
  Standing on a rail!
Jolly little fellow,
  Wiggling his tail?
Hears somebody whistling—
  Quickly runs away:
Everything seemeth lively
  At the break of day.

Golden sun appearing
  In the distant East,
Majestically rising—
  Heavens! What a feast!
Everything seemeth lovely,
  Pleasant, bright and gay—
Everything seemeth lively
  At the break of day.

TO MY LITTLE DARLING.

THE moon is shining o'er us,
   The stars are brightly gleaming;
The scene is fair before us,
   Sweet love, with bright eyes beaming.

My arms fondly enfold thee,
   With rapture to my bosom;
My eyes with joy behold thee,
   My love, my pretty blossom!

My love of loves sincerest
   From thee I ne'er will sever;
False to thee? Never, dearest!
   I must love thee forever!

And if e'er o'er my blossom
   Dark clouds threaten and lower,

I'll take thee to my bosom
 Till the angry storm is over.

I'll shield thee when in trouble,
 From tongues that idly prattle;
Though misfortunes 'round thee double,
 I'll bravely for thee battle.

And when thy heart meets sadness.
 And gloom around thee presses,
I'll win thee back to gladness
 With kisses and caresses.

But, I hear the watch-dog snarling;
 The old folks are behind us!
So kiss me good-night, darling;
 I hardly think they'll find us.

THE PIRATE'S SONG.

ABOVE me terrific thunder is crashing,
    About me the scorching lightning is flashing.
Against me the furious waves are dashing,
    But my spirit is happy and free!
Storm after storm has madly passed o'er me,
And the red jaws of hell have opened before me.
Yet my ship sailed on, as a conquerer bore me
    O'er the deep blue billowy sea:
        Let thunder crash,
        Let lightning flash,
        Let wild waves dash,
      I heed not the danger,
      To fear I am a stranger,
Life's storms can make no change in me!

I've stood on deck when the bullets were flying,
While in death my comrades around me were lying,
Till my ears were deaf with the groans of the dying,
    But my spirit was happy and free!
I have seen my enemies thicken about me,
While cutlass and knife swirled 'round and 'round me,
But I came out triumphant, no foe has yet bound me,
    As soon might they bind up the sea!

        Let bullets fly,

        Let comrades lie

        In blood, and die;

        I'll give up, no, never!

        Then on ship, forever!

Life's storms can make no change in me.

WELL-A-DAY.

ONCE I was so young and happy,
    Free and gay;
Dressed so well, so neat and flashy,
    Got good pay;
Passed away my hours of leisure,
On life's glassy sea of pleasure,
Until I fell in beyond my measure,
    Well-a-day!

Once I met a pretty fairy,
    Maggie May;
Graceful walker, stepping airy,
    Looking gay!
But the charming little kitten,
Gave one eve to me the mitten,
Strange how cruelly hearts are smitten,
    Well-a-day!

WELL=.A=DAY.

But I met another fairy,

On life's way;

Dark-eyed, rosy-faced little Mary,

Blithe and gay;

And I learned to love her dearly,

For she cherished me sincerely,

We got married—ruined nearly—

Well-a-day!

Six small fairies, with mouths like cherries,

Full of play;

But this raising little fairies,

Doesn't pay!

Sure man's life is full of trouble,

Every year his sorrows double,

Till he dies out like a bubble,

Well-a-day!

I WELCOME YOU AS A BROTHER.

LINES WRITTEN ON A YOUNG FRIEND BECOMING A MEMBER OF CENTRAL LODGE, NO. 23, OF THE I. O. O. F.

COME, Charles, my Brother, give me your hand,
 You and I have been together—
Thro' scenes of pleasure and scenes of woe,
 Thro' pleasant and gloomy weather;
But tho' many a time you and I have met
 With friendly welcome for each other,
The friendliest meeting is here to-night,
 Where "I welcome you as a Brother,"

We have stood together as faithful Knights
 Within our mystical borders;
To hold counsel for the good of all,
 To obey our Chieftain's orders;

But tho' as Companions we oft have met,
  To welcome and cheer each other,
A happier meeting is here to-night,
  Where "I welcome you as a Brother."

I have stood in the palaces of kings,
  Thro' many strange lands I've wandered;
I have slept on the blue-faced billowy sea,
  And more, fought where the cannons thundered;
But I have never before met with a scene,
  And may never meet with another
That will bring delight, as I feel to-night,
  As "I welcome you as a Brother."

Yes, Charles, you and I are Brothers now,
  And life's path looks bright before us;
But this world is so changeable, you know,
  The blue clouds that now pass o'er us,
May be followed by dark, murky clouds,
  That may divide us from each other;
But tho' my eyes see you not, my hand, Charles,
  Will know the hand of a Brother.

But let us pray to our Father above,

    And in His wisdom He'll guide us :

And you know that, if we are true to Him,

    No cloud can ever divide us ;

If we faithfully stand up for the right,

    And always do unto others,

As we would have others do unto us,

    We will live and die as Brothers,

    JUNE, 15, 1871.

EPIGRAM.

ON A PRINTER.

WHO'S the most "hen-like" fellow we have

    in this place ?

I bet, though I don't believe in betting—

That it's Charley Lighthair, for all night he *lays*,

    And all the long day he is *setting*.

    MAY, 1869.

WOMAN'S WORK.

To go to the nearest neighbor,
  And tattle all the news;
To keep her man at labor,
  Till he's down with the blues:
To ride out like a lady,
  Leaving the house in care
Of husband and the baby,
  Both in deep despair—
    Woman's work!

To go from town to town, prattling
  Wildly about "woman's rights;"
To spend the day in tattling,
  To read the *Ledger* nights;
To make her man quit housekeeping,
  And board his stamps away;

WOMAN'S WORK.

To enjoy mornings sleeping,
  And sometimes half the day—
    Woman's work!

To keep husband to caress her,
  When he ought to be away;
To hint how he must dress her,
  When he draws his next month's pay;
To raise particular thunder,
  If he don't stick to her text;
To keep him in a wonder,
  What she's going to say next—
    Woman's work!

To invite certain ladies
  Quite often to take tea,
Bringing with them their dear babies,
  Which cry distressedly;
To make her man hear the clatter
  Of her knowing female friends,

6

WOMAN'S WORK.

Till he wishes Satan had her
 In his kingdom without ends—
  Woman's work!

To go quite often shopping,
 While her man is at work;
At each dry goods store stopping,
 Smiling, talking with each clerk;
To keep up with the fashion,
 Making of herself a fool;
To fall into a passion,
 When she finds she cannot rule—
  Woman's Work!

Ah! fickle-minded woman,
 How long will it thus be,
That you'll act so inhuman,
 So simple, foolishly?
You are fair and lovely, beauty
 Is beaming from your eyes;

WOMAN'S WORK.

If you would but do your duty,
    Earth would be a paradise.

If you'd stop your silly chatter,
    (Woman's favorite delight,)
Your everlasting clatter,
    Which you keep up day and night,
You'd find this world more pleasant.
    Your home would be more blest
With contentment, than at present,
    While you give your tongue no rest.

JUNE 27, 1870.

A PRACTICAL BLESSING.

HERE we sit before a table,
    Loaded with meats fresh and sweet:
Let us eat while we are able,
    And, O Lord! bless us while we eat.

GONE.

I.

SHE has gone, yes, gone forever,
Far beyond the lethean river,
To that beautiful, enchanting, bright celestial world
above—
Where the angels meet in beauty,
To perform their holy duty,
Gathering 'round the throne of Heaven, caroling
sweet lays of love.

II.

Oh! 'twas hard to see her going
From our household, little knowing
When again we'd meet our darling, as we watch'd
her slowly die;

When again we'd hear her singing,

Melodies that still are ringing

In our ears as clear, delightful, as in happy hours

gone by.

III.

Ne'er again we'll hear her calling,

As the evening dews are falling—

" Mother, lead me to my chamber, kneel beside me

while I pray;

While I pray to blessed Jesus,

Who died that He might receive us

In that land unknown to darkness, land of bright

eternal day."

IV.

Ah! our eyes are sadly weeping,

For in death she now lies sleeping;

'Neath the green sod we have placed her, to rest

forevermore.

Ah! our hearts will sadly miss her,

And our love will long to kiss her,

But we'll kiss no more our darling, her short, sweet

life is o'er.

v.

She has gone, yea, gone forever,

Far beyond the lethean river,

To that beautiful and happy home beyond the azure

skies,

With bright angels' voices ringing,

Thro' the realms of Heaven singing.

Blessed are the good and faithful, for of such is

Paradise.

JAN. 28, 1871.

THE ANSWER.

[One evening, while at a revival, a number of my Christian friends requested me to go forward and kneel at the "altar of God." I did not feel like going forward; and as I am but a boy without even a common education, and unqualified to reason with the learned, I was unable to tell them why I refused their kind offer. After they had left me, to continue the exercise of the evening, I composed the following in answer]:

I.

WHEN thro' the dismal streets I wandered,
　　Without a friend to guide me,—
A little rag-clad beggar,
　　Without a kind one near me;
When man deem'd himself too noble,
　　To even walk beside me—
I knelt and prayed in silence,
　　And Jesus came to cheer me.

When I stood on the field of battle,
 Where Hell ope'd wide before me,
And the wild clash of bayonets
 Was ringing around me :
I looked. and lo! in the Heavens
 I saw angels hovering o'er me ;
I felt safe, for I knew Jesus
 Would ne'er let foes surround me.

III.

And when life's darkest storm was working
 It's best to terrify me ;
When the world saw me forsaken,
 Yea, lost in my own sadness;
When even the godliest mortal
 Spoke sneeringly to try me,
Christ came, and with words endearing
 He filled my soul with gladness.

IV.

Now, as I sit within the temple
    Of the God who dwells above me,
Kind Christians gather 'round me
    To warn my soul of dangers—
To tell me I am lost forever,
    If Jesus does not love me ;
Beg me kneel before the altar,
    As if Christ and I were strangers.

V.

Kind Christians and holy ministers,
    Go unto them who need ye :
The poor, the hungry beggars,
    The wretched and forsaken ;
Show them the road to happiness,
    I know that they will heed ye ;
And Christ will bless your labors,
    And their spirits he'll awaken.

7

VI.

But leave me, for I am contented—
  Yea, I care not if to-morrow
Finds me in silence resting
  My head on death's cold pillow;
I know my soul will be accepted
  In that land unknown to sorrow,
While kind friends will bury my remains
  Beneath the weeping willow.

FEB. 14, 1871.

EPIGRAM.

ON A D. D.

HE pointed to the Crucifixion' and sternly
    preached
Damnation unto all who were unbaptized;
And I stepped behind him, while his doctrine he
    taught,
And lo! *Satan was holding up the dead Christ!*

HANS FRITZ'S BEAR STORY.

VON summer day, so cool and mild,
   I valked in voods so werry vild;
And tere I sees von mighty pear,
Whose eyes at me did vildly stare.

Says I, Hans Fritz, vot vill you do?
If you stay here de pear eat you;
And if you run, de pear he run;
Py tam! I tinks dis pees no fun.

I looks and looks to see if I
Could see some friend a coming nigh,
But not a friend could I then see,
And still de pear stares vild at me.

Vhen de pig pear shakes his pig head,
I tinks I now vill soon pe dead;

Then de pig pear jumps right for me,
And then Hans Fritz goes for a tree.

De pear he coomes, and up I goes
Von pig oak tree; for vell I knows
That if de pear gets hold of me,
I nevermore Hans Fritz will pe.

Mine Got! Mine Got! Vot do I see?
Dat savage pear coomes up de tree!
I tinks, alas! my tays are o'er!
Von Dutchman soon vill pe no more.

Now on a limb, now up de tree,
And still de pear does follow me.
Golly! I tinks I'se got someting;
Yes—in my pouch tere pees von string.

So now I vill tie it around
Dis pig oak limb I knows pe sound;
I does it quick, for vell I knows
De pig-mouthed pear pees werry close.

I gets it tied, and den I takes
A hold of it; py tam, it preaks!
Down, down I goes, vay down de tree!
I tinks Hans Fritz vill cease to pe.

I hits de ground mit feet and head,
Tunder and blixen! and yet not dead?
It hurts me so I gives von schream,
I vake, and lo! it's but a dream!

Kind friends, von tings I vish to say:
Let *lager peer* alone at day;
For if you trinks as oft I do,
A pig-mouthed pear may coome to you.
JULY, 1869.

EPITAPH—ON A LIAR.

SING and be merry; for here lies
The greatest liar 'neath the skies:
On earth he served his *Father* well,
So now he lives with him in Hell.

BUGGY RIDING.

———

OH ! give me a ride, a buggy ride,
    With my sweet little darling by my side—
My blithe little girl with a rosy cheek,
And not afraid now and then to speak,
Nor afraid of being fondly entwined
By an arm that lazily lingers behind.
      What a joy it is,
      What elysian bliss,
I feel when out riding with my pretty miss!

O, you city chaps, so lively and gay!
You may sing of promenades up Broadway;
Of fine Sunday afternoons at the Park;
Of open-air concerts after dark;
Of operas grand, where you oftentimes meet:

And festive saloons, where sweet danties you eat:

    It's all very nice,

    Especially the price

That you pay to make earth a paradise.

Prize the enjoyments that make your hours flee,

For scant the delight they furnish for me;

But give me an occasional buggy ride,

With my sweet little darling by my side;

Then hurrah for fun as away we go,

Over hills and glens, riding to and fro,

    Happy are we,

    And jolly and free,

As we dash o'er the highway so merrily.

And she sings to me, my sweetest of girls,

With sparkling dark eyes and auburn curls,

Enchanting my heart with sweet melodies,

As we slowly ride 'gainst the soft, cool breeze;

And her coral lips meet mine with a kiss,

As I draw her closer, the sweet little miss :
 And the moon gives light,
 And the stars shine bright,
As we leisurely take our homeward flight.

Seasons may come, and seasons may go,
And life see scenes of pleasure or woe ;
But where'er I am, and whate'er I see,
Nothing will give as much pleasure to me
As on a starry night a buggy ride,
With my own fair darling sitting by my side,
 Alone and free,
 Jolly lovers are we,
As we dash o'er the highway so merrily.

TO A DEAD COMRADE.

REST, comrade, rest; Ah! I think of thee sadly,
    I think of the days when I was with thee:
When together we went to battle-field gladly,
    To fight for our home, the land of the free;
I little then dreamed the close of the battle
    Would find thee numbered among the slain;
That the clash of arms, the cannon's loud rattle,
    Would bring thee to me never again.

Memory brings back the night I found thee lying,
    Wounded, bleeding, so bravely waiting for death;
Memory, must I again see him dying?
    Again feel my comrade's last suffering breath?
Again hear him speak of his sorrowing mother,
    Who had gone before him to realms above?

8

Again hear him speak with sobs of another,—
    The bright-eyed maiden who cherished his love ?

I see again thy bright hazel eyes beaming.
    Comrade, I see again that face of thine ;
The same golden stars that were o'er us gleaming,
    Are gleaming to-night in their beauty divine ;
But thou art no more ; the green sod lies o'er thee,
    Thy spirit dwells now in Heaven above,
With her who went there long, long years before
      thee,
    To chant with the angels carols of love.

Rest, comrade, rest ; sadly o'er me are creeping
    Memories of thee, thou so noble and brave ;
Gladly I would that 'twas I who was sleeping—
    That thou wert living, and I in thy grave ;
That earth's fondest hopes around thee were clinging,
    That life with its joys gave pleasure to thee ;
O! 'twould be bliss, wert thou here to-night singing
    Sweet happy songs as thou oft sang to me.

Rest, comrade, rest; thy bright days are o'er,

The cold, mouldering clay now forms thy bed;

In dreams o'er thy grave sings thy comrade rover,

And weeps, sadly weeps o'er the grave of the
dead.

Thy land may forget thee—forget thou did'st ever

Fall for the cause of the noble and free :—

But, comrade, while life lasts, forget thee I'll never;

Memory will ever blend life's past with thee.

May 30, 1870.

EPIGRAM.

ON A YOUNG LADY WHO CLAIMS TO BE THE "BELLE OF THE CITY."

IF "Beauty" is made by "Virtue" alone,

I'm sorry to say 'tis little you own;

But if "Folly" and "Paint" can make one pretty,

Then truly you are the *Belle of the City*.

EVERY DAY.

THIS world is growing faster
    Every day;
There's nothing e'er will pass her,
    So they say;
But I'll bet my " apple-grinder,"
(That is, if I can find her,)
That to-morrow will leave behind her
    Yesterday.

This world is growing wiser
    Every day;
Scientific men revise her
    Every day;
Population is growing bigger,
Giving more work for Death's digger—

EVERY DAY. ·

More respect paid to the "nigger,"
    Every day.

This world is growing keener
    Every day;
All but Greely—she grows greener
    Every day;
Och, begorra! 'tis alarming
What that "old girl knows 'bout farming,"
And tells it to us in such a charming,
    Graceful way.

This world is growing wickeder
    Every day,
Tho' Beecher gets a lick at her
    Every day;
Yet "Christianity" is fading,
Folks are tired of "pilgrim raiding,"
Tired of church promenading
    Every day.

This world is growing prouder
Every day;
"Female roosters" crowing louder
Every day;
Aristocrats are growing lazier,
Politicians are growing crazier,
Making things grow somewhat hazier
Every day.

This world is growing drearier
Every day;
Many are growing wearier
Every day;
Many leave this world of evil,
And I'm thinking on the level
Many are going to the Devil
Every day.'

JULY 14, 1870.

DISOWNED.

———

DARKNESS surrounding me,
Dark thoughts confounding me,
Filling me with anguish;
Cast out, disowned; ah me!
Friendless, unknown; ah me!
Left here alone; ah me!
In pain to languish.

Though many pray for me,
Not any stay for me,
To cheer and befriend me;
Oh! what are prayers to me
When no one cares for me,
When no one dares for me
To speak, and defend me?

True worldly charity
Is really a rarity
    To a lost woman ;
Never befriending her,
Kindly attending her,
But ready. for sending her
    To hells inhuman.

But though earth's no peace for me,
The Savior has ease for me
    Stored up in Heaven ;
Though unprotected here,
Scorned and rejected here,
I'll be accepted there—
    Welcome and forgiven.

FOLLOW ME.

A DEEP spell of sadness has come o'er me,
  'The merriment of my soul has fled;
My heart, once so light, now beats wretchedly,
  And silently longs for the dead.
For whene'er I mingle in the gay crowd,
  I hear above its mirth—wild and free—
A sweet mystic voice, and it crieth aloud:
  Follow me! follow me! follow me!

And when glitt'ring stars in the heavens shine
  So brightly on the face of earth;
And the babbling brooklets in sweet notes chime
  With the nightingale's charming mirth;
Then, as in my silent chamber I lie
  Entranced by nature's melody,

9

I'm startled by that low mystical cry:
Follow me! follow me! follow me!

O, Father of Light! What meaneth these words
That haunt my ears each day and night?
So soft, yet as sweet as the musical birds
That charm me with songs of delight
Can it be some one in that wondrous land,
Where spirits bask happy and free!
Can it be I'm wanted by one of that band,
Who crieth : follow me! follow me!

Perchance it is she who once made life so dear—
My mother, whose soul went above,
To that home ever free from sorrow and fear,
That kingdom of eternal love;
But loving me so well, she has left that shore,
To guide me o'er life's troubled sea;
O! is it my mother who crieth o'er and o'er :
Follow me! follow me! follow me?

To-night I'm among the blithe and gay,

Whose faces look happy and glad;

Kind friends request me to join in play,

But my heart is too wretched and sad;

For above the voices of the festive crowd—

Above their notes of innocent glee—

I hear that strange voice, and it calleth aloud:

Follow me! follow me! follow me!

SEPT. 7, 1872.

EPIGRAM.

"ARE you a Lawyer?" "Yes, sir." "Have
much practice?"

"Oh! yes; for I'm well versed in Blackstone."

"Are you? Well, good-day; I want a man
Who depends upon *brains* and *backbone*."

Beautiful,
Dutiful,
Noble and sincere;
Speaks cheering;
Endearing,
Delicious and clear.

Not antic,
Not frantic,
Not wasting his time;
Advancing,
Not dancing
Away every dime.

He drinks not,
Nor shrinks not

From doing what's right :

He swears not,

Nor scares not

Young girls into fright.

Tho' fearless,

Not cheerless,

But happy and gay :

Tho' stainless,

Not brainless,

But reasons alway.

Ambitious,

Judicious,

He knows how to plan :

Moves sprightly,

Acts rightly—

A true gentleman.

AN HYMENEAN ODE.

WILLIAM, my boy!
I understand you'll be married to-night;
Well, I wish you joy,
And I hope that your future life will be bright.
But mark my word, the step that you take to-night
Will be either the brightest or darkest of your life;
So be careful and sure that you are right,
And if so, go ahead, and make her a happy wife.
You have coo'd her,
Fairly woo'd her,
Now 'tis right for you to take her
In holy companionship for life.
But listen to me, O, delighted lad!
Don't you ever in life forsake her,
Or with a man's coldness make her sad;

Or with unreasonable words break her

Heart; a woman's heart is tender,

  And one angry frown

  Can easily strike down

To sickness and death her form so slender;

  So be kind to your wife

  All the days of her life,

And blind to her faults—that is if she has any,

And you know some women have got a good many;

  But then some men are no better off—

And oft get on a tremendous big bender !

  Just to get rid of a harmless cough.

Matrimonial life is not all honey,

Nor so exceedingly funny,

As some young folks believe it to be;

And a man not overstocked with money

  Cannot be too wary

  Who he's going to mary,

For a good many women are rather free—

  About this and that,

  And each new style hat,

Dasher, Corset, and God only knows what!

Are daily and hourly anxiously sought,

And, tho' you must borrow, they must be bought:

> And if you can't buy,

> Why then she'll cry,

And in murmurs rather unmusical she'll tell you

That she's sorry she didn't marry Joe Joker,

Charles Croaker, or even a *real estate broker*,

Than such a stupid fellow.

> But, my boy, take her!

> I know you'll ne'er make her

Feel as if she had married the wrong fellow.

> May your heart grow lighter,

> And your path grow brighter

Each day, as your life grows more ripe and mellow;

> May misfortune never

> Come to you, but ever

May fortune bless you with life's sweetest joys;

> May your home be lighten'd,

> Yea, alarmingly brighten'd

With "Love's dearest tokens"—*girls and boys*.

———

LIVELIEST and merriest
    Girl in the west;
Thy lips the cherriest
    Lips ever pressed.

Thy teeth the pearliest,
    By nature well set;
Thy locks the curliest
    Locks fingered yet.

Thy eyes the queenliest
    Beneath the skies;
Even the sereneliest
    Are won by thine eyes.

Thy heart the cheeriest
    Of hearts on earth;

10

Winning the weariest
　　With its sweet mirth.

Thy love the holiest,
　　Brought from above;
And I, the lowliest,
　　Have won that love.

Life, sweetest, coziest,
　　Blessings be thine;
Girl of girls rosiest!
　　Sweetheart of mine.

LINES ON KISSING KATE.

SAYS I to dark-eyed Kate, " How do you like this?"
　　As on her coral lips I 'printed a kiss;
" How do I like it, Johnny? The truth is this—
I would like it if you 'd take back the kiss."

WAITING FOR THE STAGE.

LINES WRITTEN IN A BAR ROOM OF A WESTERN
TAVERN.

ALL 'round me are sitting
    Old topers, who 're hitting
Each other with their low humorous jokes ;
    But bless me what swearing,
    Christ's name little sparing,
For themselves little caring,—what impious folks !

    Ah ! just hear them lying,
    I guess they are trying
To beat Beelzebub. Well, topers, go it;
    If you don't get damn'd in—
    Yes, and get well cramm'd in—
To Tartarus, then I am no poet.

Sights horribly shocking!

Haloo! what's that knocking,

Kicking 'gainst the door? 'nother toper? All right;

What! coming in tripping?

Surely he's been sipping.

Haloo! down? Come, topers, raise him, he's tight.

Been out all night helling,

Pell melling, selling

His soul to Satan for a draught of gin;

Children at home crying

For bread, poor wife dying,

He hanging 'round hell holes with companions in sin.

"Hey, thar, you cuss writin';

"Bet you take delight in

Composin'; hey, don't you, you young chap?

Look out—too much thinkin'

Wunce sot me to drinkin',

And run thro' a fortune like a thunder clap."

"Silence, wretched being!

You'll soon be seeing

The horrors of —" "Bet you mean hell; don't you,

bub?

Swar, that's sassy talkin',

Boy; set you to walkin'

Out o' this room, you little black-eyed cub!"

*   *   *   *   *   *

Halloo! What! Stage nighing?

Yes; hurrah! I'm dying

To get away from this terrible crew."

" Passengers?"   "One."   "Get in!

No seat, hey? Well sit in

That colored gal's lap, guess she won't charm you!"

THE LOVER'S PLEA.

1.

O, ENTREAT me not to leave thee,
   I will ne'er in life deceive thee,
But I will brighten thy future,
   If thou wilt but give to me
The heart I so fondly cherish;
Without it I surely must perish,
For my happiness, yea, my very
   Life is centered all in thee.

I have loved thee, loved thee madly!
Yea, I love thee still, and gladly
I'd enfold thee to my bosom,
   As in the Elysian days!
When thy presence wildly thrilled me,
And thy notes of gladness filled me,

As I loved to look and linger
  O'er thy happy, pleasant ways.

Thou didst call me then thy dearest,
Well I know I was the nearest
To thy heart. O, tell me, fairest,
  Carest thou no more for me?
Hast thou cast me off forever,
With the determination never
Again to know me as thy lover—
  As the dearest one to thee?

II.

Thou sayest that I will not love thee
When sorrow's clouds hang above thee;
That I'll seek the charms of others
  When thy beauties pass away;
That my love for thee will grow colder
As each day sees thee grow older;
And the promises be broken
  That I gave thee yesterday.

O! believe me, I'll adore thee
When the darkest clouds hang o'er thee;
I will clear the way before thee,
    And make cheerful thy life's strife;
When sorrows and pains assail thee,
Yea, and even thy senses fail thee.
Thou wilt find me near to guide thee
    Safely through the trials of life.

III.

O! entreat me not to leave thee,
For my arms would fain receive thee,
My quivering lips are burning
    To be pressed to thine again;
My heart is wildly beating
To receive 'gain thy heart's greeting:
O dearest! why dost thou linger?
    Why thus keep me in this pain?

Come again to me, O thou fairest
Of maidens! I know thou carest

Still for me. Thy bright, beautiful
  Hazel eyes speak love to me.
Thy cheeks are aglow. Thy lips burning
Like my own, for the returning
Of the olden love, that so often
  Madden'd our hearts with glee.

IV.

Mine, mine again! O the gladness
I feel now! the spell of sadness
Has left me, gone, gone forever,
  And I am happy once more ;
My sweetheart has returned, and dearer
She seemeth to me, yea, nearer
Unto my heart; and brighter, clearer,
  Shineth her eyes than e'er before.

Mine, mine again ! O never,
My own, my darling, will we sever

Again. We'll part from each other
 Ne'er again till life is o'er.
Thank heaven! I again enfold thee
To my heart; again behold thee
Reclining thy head on my bosom,
 Mine, mine forevermore!

EPIGRAM.

ON A TEACHER WHO HAS A HABIT OF LECTURING
HIS SCHOOL.

A TEACHER while giving a lecture to his school,
 Asked a small boy if he came there to play the
  fool;
The thoughtless boy replied: "No, Sir-ee, kind
  teacher,
Nor did I come here to hear a *dull preacher.*"

OUR POETS.

IF a great man dies, our poets all
   See him to Heaven's portal;
Ten thousand bards will sing his praise,
   And make his name immortal;
They'll swear by all that is divine,
   He was the nation's glory;
They'll stamp his name in blank verse line,
   And leave us read the story.

If a poor wretch dies, our poets all
   See him to Nick's dominions;
Ten thousand bards will use their brains
   To blacken his opinions;
Triumphantly they'll dedicate
   Their lays to the All-seeing;

Yea, wear the cloak of the righteous
   To damn their fellow-being.

But poets are a mystic set,
   And oft sing very queerly;
Sometimes they'll praise their enemies,
   And curse their friends sincerely.
They do not deem it necessary
   To sing always in reason,
But, as a general thing, you'll hear
   Them sing in every season.

.

In olden times the poet's strain
   Was full of manly passion;
But now-a-days the poet's strain
   Is soften'd to the fashion;
He sings in fear of being censured
   By some poor hungry writer,
Who censures others to save himself
   From growing somewhat lighter.

Ah, me! if ever in lifetime, I
    Turn out to be a poet,
I hope and pray that common sense
    Will mark my lines to show it;
That the songs I'll sing will be written
    In simple English letters,
And that I'll never try to ape,
    Or trifle with my betters.

EPIGRAM.

ON A BEAUTIFUL GIRL.

THAT thou art beautiful, no one dare deny;
    No fairer maiden lives beneath the sky;
I would take thee for an angel, thou art so sweet,
If I but knew that angels were full of conceit.

ISADORE.

LIFE seemeth dreary,
   Wretchedly weary,
No sweet smiles to cheer me, heart sad and sore;
   Silent and lonely,
   Ah! thinking only
Of my little darling, sweet Isadore.

   Were I but near her,
   Could I but hear her
Singing sweet melodies, as in days of yore;
   When as a glad lover,
   I walked through the clover
With my companion rover, dear Isadore.

   Bright scenes of pleasure,
   Sweet hours of leisure,
Earth's rarest treasure, can not restore—

She who was dearest,

Truest, sincerest,

Affectionately nearest, fair Isadore.

All that I live for,

Earnestly strive for,

Hope for, contrive for, is nothing more—

Then when this life ends,

This saddened strife ends,

I will be nearer to my Isadore.

Spirit immortal!

At heaven's portal

I know thou'rt waiting, to greet me once more;

I'll soon reach the river,

Where we'll join forever,

To part again never, beloved Isadore!

THE PRISONER.

* * * MEMORY is stealing o'er me,
The scenes I cherished in the days of yore
Come back again: the hills, the dells—I see
The gleaming blue-faced lake, the pebbled shore,
Where oft I stood, but, ah! will stand no more.

I see again the old cottage; 'gain hear
My mother's glowing words; her voice so clear
'Gain cheers me. She kisses me; bidst me play
With her—who forever I must hold dear,
My childhood companion—little sister Ida!
She comes with smiles that win me like a charm;
Her sparkling eyes with rapturous joy now beam,
As off we go, merrily, arm in arm,
To play on the banks of some crystal stream;
O, Christ! let me die in this beautiful dream.

Ah! the dream changes: O, horrors! I see
My father staggering—reeling towards me;
I see the tears in mother's eyes; Ida!
Ida! come here to me. O, what shall we do!
Where shall we go to keep out o' his way?
Come Ida: quick, quick! he'll strike you. There,
    there!
He's striking mother! She reels! she falls! See,
See! Ida! Ida! he's coming here! Where
Can we go? He comes! he comes! O, Heaven be
With us. Great God! why comes this dream to me?

      *   *   *   *   *

Farewell, Friendship; thou'st ne'er been true to me;
I only found thee 'mid scenes of pleasure,
When Fortune sang to me her melody.
When life's storms found me without a treasure—
Homeless—when I cried to thee from the bed
Of pain and sickness, thou didst not hear me;
No feathery pillow placed thou 'neath my head;

No glowing words spakest thou to cheer me.
Curst be thee! thou didst not e'en come near me.

Ha! ha! I'm free at last! The mystic spell
That held me so long in the bonds of slavery
Has been broken. Thou art a child of Hell,
Friendship! Cunning, well versed in knavery—
A hypocrite. Thou'st been a curse to me;
False and deceiving. 'Tis well we sever:
Flattery, mockery, I've only found in thee.
Thou'st fool'd me often, but never, never
Will I again trust thee. Farewell, forever.

    *   *   *   *   *

Ye glittering stars! how fair ye shine to-night;
And O, thou beauteous moon! thy sweet light
Is peeping thro' these iron bars near me.
How silent is the night—how clear and bright!
I hear nothing, and naught cares to hear me.
Shunned by all, as if the world did fear me;

Alone in chains! Ah, me! the cursed spell
That brought me here—allowed men to steer me
Within these walls—within this dark, cold cell.
This gloomy, dreary, solitary hell!

And thou, so slow, O, Time! passing so slow;
Keeping my soul in bondage, in this woe
So torturing—this uncontrollable pain!
Was I to blame? They say I was. Then so
Be it. Will this deep sanguinary stain
Of my dark crime forever haunt my brain?
Must I live here, and never, never hear
The sweetness of a friendly voice again?
Must I feel this torture year after year?
Live, die in hell, and Paradise so near?

Am I dead to thee, O, Christ? Thou who sought
The prisoner in his lonely cell; taught
Him to feel the enchantment of thy love—
Am I dead to thee? Canst thou not be brought

By prayer from thy celestial throne above
Into this darkened cell ?   Dost thou, too, reprove
My soul ? thou, too, doom it to endless misery ?
Am I so harden'd that I cannot move
The divine, compassionate love in thee ?
Canst thou be Christ and have no love for me ?

What ! am I lost ?   Will I ne'er feel the bliss
Of Heaven ? Ne'er feel the joys above this
World of sin ?   What ! never ?   Is my destiny
Hell ? Into that dark fathomless abyss
Of sin and crime ?   Into that misery
Eternal ?   Into that unquenchable sea
Of fire ?   Is there my future—is it there ?
Ah ! it comes before my eyes; See ! see ! Ye
Infernal fiends ! why come ye here ?   How dare
Ye come ?   Away ! mock me not with your stare !

Away, ye fiends !   Why at me now ?   Am I
Not harden'd yet ?   Am I not fit for hell ?   Why

Test me again? O. horrors! hear the groans
Of tortured victims! Ah! see them lie
Bleeding and in chains! Hear the mocking moans
Of the madden'd demons, in deep, wild tones!
See them hurl their victims into the hot mire!
Now see the devils dance! What! are they stones?
Have they no hearts, no love, no humane desire?
Fearfully reveling amidst Jehovah's fire!

Cries, cries! horrible cries assail my ears!
I see her! see her! My murdered victim appears
Before me! Hear her pleading for mercy;
Ah! see her stare with eyes swollen with tears;
Horrors! see her white arms stretched out to me,
Begging for life! O, woe! O, misery!
Take me, ye demons! take me out of this cell;
Satan, I'm thine! Hear, hear, I call on thee!
Torture me—rack me with the pains of Hell;
Do what thou wilt, but break this madd'ning spell.

Listen ! What's that ? My soul, they come ! they
   come !
The demons come to take thee to thy home !
See, see ! No, no ! O, heavens ! What is this
Pale skeleton doing here ? Speak ! speak ! What !
   dumb ?
Hast thou nothing to say ? What is thy office ?
Away, fiend ! What ! move not for me ! What is
Thy want ? Speak, devil, speak ! Come, come, un-
   sheath
Thy tongue. Com'st thou from the dark abyss
Of sin ? Hold, hold ! I know thee—my breath !
Ha ! ha ! I know thee now—'tis Death ! Death !
   Death !

THE CHIEFTAIN.

———

STEADY, there, steady! their columns are nighing;
Whiz!

Whiz!

Whiz!

·Good heavens! they're at us!
Already the lead is whistling, flying;
Jove! I hope none of their balls will spat us;
Lay us low before we can combat them;
Have patience. my boys, we'll soon get at them.
Ha! see how proudly their flags are waving;
Hold your fire. there. hold your fire!
We'll soon set the proud devils to raving.
Let them shout. and raise their flags higher,
We'll soon give them more than they desire.

Steady, there, steady! by Jove! what do you mean,

Firing at them at the distance they are?

Let them come nearer, as near as they dare,

Let their thick columns so proud and serene,

Come nearer and nearer, we'll soon change the scene;

We'll soon spoil the harmony of their thunder.

How slowly they're coming,

How their balls are humming.

Whiz!

Whiz! whiz!

They're having their fun,

But before the setting of yonder sun,

Before to-day's bloody work is done,

Those thick ranks will be scattered asunder.

Now, boys, get ready!

Fire!

Fire!

Let your steel ring now,

Make your guns sing now,

Let loose the pieces, let them rattle!

The louder and deeper the dire

The more wild and terrific the battle.

Steady, boys, steady!

You 're wasting fire.   Shoot lower!

Lower!

      Lower!

         Make legs the score;

Give them your lead while they 're crossing the

      clover;

Let the field be drenched with the enemy's gore.

That's it! tumble them over and over!

We 'll soon see the whole pack of them lying

Scattered here and there on the blood-stained field;

Let them lie—

      Let them die—

         What care we for their dying,

They came to conquer but we 'll make them yield.

Now, tigers, for them, give it to them!
Let your steel ring and sting, hew them
Down, like the furious hurricane sweeps down
The forest. Hurrah! they 're at a stand!
Away!
      Away!
Over the works, boys, over the works!
Close in on them, fight them hand to hand,
Down on them, like the lion leaps down
On its prey. Into them like a legion of Turks
Thirsting for the blood of a Christian land.

      Yelling, screaming,

      Bayonets gleaming,

      Proud flags streaming,

         About and o'er us;

      Bullets flying,

      Wounded sighing,

      And dead lying

         Behind and before us.

Heavens! what a terrible conflict this is,
How the lead whistles and flies and hisses,
How coolly it lays on the grassy level
Many a poor but brave mortal devil.

    All Hell is gushing
       From the womb of Earth!
    Triumphantly flushing
       In its maddened mirth;
And Earth, Mother Earth, is mad with herself,
Her children have broke into wild sedition;
One half is fighting the other half for Pelf,
Whilst the other half is fighting for Ambition.

Hurrah!
      There they go!
Flying!
      Flying!
Now for them, braves, drive them into the river;
Man! don't stop for him—what if he is dying!

Would you have a man live here forever?

Man was born to die—

Away!

Away!

Push on, my braves, push ahead, push ahead!

Over the wounded and over the dead.

If my brother fell I'd not stop.   What is

A thousand deaths to a victory like this?

Down on them, braves, down, down on your prey.

That's it, push ahead! ha! this is glorious!

The enemy flying and we again victorious!

ZELAIDE.

OF all the girls that live in town,
  There is none like Zelaide.
She is the best, up street or down,
  In sunshine or in shade;
Go where you will, o'er vale or hill,
  She's fairest 'mong the girls;
With eyes so blue, and lips—for who?—
  And, oh! what handsome curls.

Ofttimes I wish that I could kiss
  Beautiful Zelaide;
For 'sooth she is a handsome miss,
  That very same sweet maid.
And if I live, truly I'll strive
  To win her for my wife;
But if I fail, sadly I'll wail,
  And lone will be my life.

RUSTICATING.

RUSTICATING.

O UT a rusticating,
   Where cool breezes blow
Thro' the sylvan bowers,
   Lightly to and fro;
Passing summer hours
   Joyously away,
Where everything is pleasant,
   Lively, bright and gay.

Out a rusticating,
   Where my Birdie dwells,
My little bonnie lassie,
   Fairest of rural belles;
Came out here to woo her,
   And win her if I can—

RUSTICATING.

For oh! I love her dearly,
   If there is love in man.

Out a rusticating,
   Having lots of fun,
While city chaps are grumbling
   Under that hot sun,
Here I am enjoying
   The sweetest spells of life;
Love and fun together,
   Free from care and strife.

Skipping thro' the clover,
   Tripping over hills,
Dashing thro' the woodlands,
   Splashing thro' the rills;
Prancing thro' the garden,
   Dancing in the barn,
Yelling at the cattle, ·
   Telling some big yarn.

RUSTICATING.

Chasing after roosters,
    Racing with the dogs,
Pushing thro' the bushes,
    Rushing over logs;
Climbing over fences,
    Rhyming in the shade,
Lying in some bower,
    Trying a promenade.

Straying thro' the orchard,
    Playing 'neath the trees,
Swinging in the back-yard,
    Singing songs to please;
Annoying the hired hands,
    Enjoying their fun,
They're the jolliest fellows
    Living 'neath the sun.

Walking down the highway,
    Meeting country girls;

RUSTICATING.

Pretty bonnie lasses,
  Bright as ocean pearls;
Innocent and modest,
  Who does not love them?
Fascinating creatures!
  Every one a gem.

Pretty bonnie lasses!
  Healthy, pure and neat;
Manners rather simple,
  Yet charming and sweet;
A la Paris fashions
  Will not do for them;
Fascinating creatures,
  Every one a gem.

Pretty bonnie lasses!
  Dressed in calico.
When they meet a fellow,
  How their hearts aglow:

RUSTICATING.

How their faces redden
    When one speaks to them :
Fascinating creatures,
    Every one a gem.

*   *   *   *   *   *   *

Hallo! there's my Birdie!
    Tripping lightly along:
Merriest of maidens,
    Full of life and song.
Ha! her eyes behold me,
    Now her heart's in glee :
Quicken steps, my Birdie,
    Hasten, sweet, to me.

Prettiest bonnie lassie
    Living in this place;
Happy smiles are always
    Playing on your face;

RUSTICATING.

May misfortune never
  Cross your life's pathway;
God grant that you may ever
  Be blithesome and gay.

Arm in arm together
  Slowly let us walk—
Down into the garden,
  And there we'll have a talk;
We'll pass away the moments,
  Pass away the hours,
Resting cozily in
  Nature's fairest bow'rs.

Birdie, while we trip along
  Carol some melody;
Carol, sweet nightingale,
  Songs so dear to me;
Your happy melodies
  Make my heart rejoice,

For truly, there's nothing
  So charming as your voice.

SONG—"IF YOU'LL BE TRUE TO ME."

" I'll follow you, I'll follow you,
  Wherever you may go—
Over the mountains bright and blue,
  And over mountains of snow.
No odds how dark may be the strife,
  I'll ever faithful be;
I'll fondly cling to you through life,
  If you'll be true to me.

" I'll follow you, I'll follow you,
  With you I'll e'er abide;
You'll find your sweetheart ever true
  And ever by your side.
My thoughts, my love, my heart, are thine,
  And evermore will be;

I'll trust with you all that is mine,
If you'll be true to me."

Ha! that is charming!
Quite a song indeed :
Now sing another one
While slowly we proceed ;
You know I love to hear
Those molodies of thine ;
They thrill me with their sweetness
And harmony divine.

SONG—"BIRDIE'S FAVORITE."

"Oh! I love a certain fellow!
He's as sweet as sweet can be ;
But his name I will not tell you,
For it is too dear to me ;
Yet altho' my heart he's taken,
He knows not that it is his ;

Oh! I would that I could awaken
His young heart with love's sweet kiss.

"Oh, he's just as neat and pretty
As ever a lad can be,
And you'll not find one more witty
Than the one so dear to me;
Yet, altho' he meets me often,
He claims me not yet as his.
Oh! I would that I could soften
His young heart with love's sweet kiss.

"Oh, I love him, love him dearly!
He is all this world to me,
And if he loves not sincerely,
What a sad life mine will be.
Oh, I wish that he would tell me
Words that would thrill me with bliss—
Tell me that he loves me dearly,
For I am already his."

RUSTICATING.

Birdie, of all the song birds
　You are the sweetest bird;
Your voice is far the clearest,
　Finest I've ever heard.
Your songs fill me with gladness,
　They fill my heart with glee;
They awaken old memories,
And bring dear thoughts to me.

　　　．

Halloo! here's the garden,
　Here the bee reposes;
Here, my bonnie lassie,
　We'll rest among the roses;
While Nature's sweet songsters
　Will flit 'bout and o'er us,
Chanting their wild carols,
　Ringing loud the chorus.

Flowers sweetly blooming—
　Well may we be joyous

RUSTICATING.

Resting 'mong the roses,
   With nought to annoy us,
I will wreathe some flowers
   In your auburn tresses,
While your dainty fingers
   Shower fond caresses.

Birdie, listen to me,
   I've a word to say:
I want a little song-bird
   To be mine alway;
To sing when I am lonely,
   To sing when I am sad;
To sing and for me only,
   To make me fore'er glad.

I want a little maiden
   Fore'er to be my own,
One who'll ever love me,
   And love me alone;

RUSTICATING.

A tender-hearted maiden,
  Full of love and cheer;
One whose ways are pleasant,
  Gentle and sincere."

I've hunted thro' cities
  And thro' country places,
Seeking for my heart's darling
  'Mong the pretty faces;
But till I met you, Birdie,
  I never met my dearest;
You are my love's first choice,
  You are my heart's nearest.

There are charms about you
  More than half divine,
And the soul within you
  Binds my soul to thine;
You have pierced my bosom
  With Love's mystic dart—

RUSTICATING.

Birdie, I do love you,
   Love you with all my heart.

Do you love me? come, now,
   Look me in the face,
Let me see your hazel eyes,
   And my fate I'll trace;
Look up, pretty Birdie,
   Will you bless my life?
Will you be my darling—
   Will you be my wife?

Dearest, will you be mine?
   Come, now, don't say no;
" Silence always gives consent,"
   So you're mine, I know.
I'll kiss away the blushes
   Blooming for me alone,
Enfold you to my bosom,
   My beautiful, my own!

RUSTICATING.

By the gods immortal!
  Birdie, you eclipse
Any of the lasses,
  With your honey lips;
Your delicious kisses
  Thrill me thro' and thro'—
What would be this wide world,
  Darling, without you?

Bosom gently heaving,
  Heart beating in its glee;
Delicate white arms clinging
  'Round my neck tenderly;
Beautiful radiant eyes
  Beaming into mine;
Penetrating into mine,
  Love, pure and divine.

Happiness Elysian?
  Paradise regained!

RUSTICATING.

This may be but a vision—
   If so. I am a saint.
Surely its enchanting,
   Sweetest joy below!
Courting 'mong the roses,—
   Birdie, ain't it so!

    *   *   *   *   *   *   *

Out a rusticating
   Summer hours away,
While city chaps are toiling
   All the live long day—
Here I am so coolly,
   Sitting in the shade,
Tenderly embracing
   My darling little maid.

Gentle breezes sweeping
   Thro' our sylvan home—

RUSTICATING.

Would'nt give a penny
   Ever 'gain to roam;
Rather in my happiness
   Linger here alone—
Gaily rusticating
   With my love, my own.

THE END.

www.ingramcontent.com/pod-product-compliance
Lightning Source LLC
Chambersburg PA
CBHW032018010726
47493CB00007B/2467